The Only One Club

Written by Jane Naliboff

Illustrated by Jeff Hopkins

Flashlight Press

New York

For my family and my dearest friend, H.K.B., with love. –JN

To my family. –JH

Thank you to D.E.N. who inspired the story, and S.D.G. who believed in it. –JN

First Edition – October 2004

Library of Congress Control Number: 2004104837

ISBN 0-972-92253-9

Editor: Shari Dash Greenspan
Graphic Design: The Virtual Paintbrush
This book was typeset in New Baskerville.
Illustrations were rendered in a medley of pencil, acrylic, watercolor and pastel.

Distributed by Independent Publishers Group

Flashlight Press • 3709 13th Avenue • Brooklyn, NY 11218
www.FlashlightPress.com

"Today we're all going to make Christmas decorations,"
Mrs. Matthews said as she handed out colored paper.
"Then we'll hang them on the classroom windows."

Jennifer Jacobs's hand shot up.
"Yes, Jennifer?" said Mrs. Matthews.

"Mrs. Matthews, I'm Jewish. I celebrate Hanukah."

"Oh," said Mrs. Matthews. "Are you the only one?"

Everyone looked around. No other hands went up.

"Well, Jennifer, it looks like you are. You can make Hanukah decorations instead."

Scissors cut.

Crayons colored.

Laughter escaped and there were giggles galore as the children turned paper into pointy trees, striped stockings, chubby gingerbread people, and lots and lots of stars.

Jennifer's star had six points instead of five.

"It's a Star of David," she explained to Olivia. "A Jewish star."

"Jennifer," said Mrs. Matthews, "you may put up your Hanukah decorations first."
Jennifer proudly marched to the middle window and taped her stars, menorah, and chain of dreidels to the glass. Then she stood back to admire her work.

One at a time, the other children put up their
decorations. The classroom looked magical, and smiles
stretched across happy faces. Then the bell rang.

Coats were grabbed.
Hats flew onto heads.
Feet jumped into boots and hands pushed into
mittens as everyone ran out the door, heading
for home.

"I'm the only one in my class who's Jewish," Jennifer announced that night at dinner. "I'm the only one who made Hanukah decorations, I'm the only one whose stars have six points instead of five, and I got to put my decorations up first."

"That must make you feel special," her father said.

After dinner Jennifer took out her art supplies. She cut out a large orange circle and carefully edged it with glitter. Then, with her favorite marker, she wrote THE ONLY ONE CLUB on it in big letters. She pinned the badge to her sweater for school the next day.

Olivia Raven noticed THE ONLY ONE CLUB badge right away.
"What's that for?" she asked.
"I'm the only one in the class who's Jewish," Jennifer explained,
"so I started a club and I'm the only one in it!" Jennifer skipped
towards the classroom with Olivia right behind her.

"Can I join?" asked Olivia.

"No," said Jennifer, "you celebrate Christmas."

"So? That's not what your badge says. It says THE ONLY ONE CLUB and I'm the only one in the class whose last name is a kind of bird."

Jennifer stopped skipping and turned away. She wasn't sure what to say.

Jonah noticed the glittery badge during lunch.

"What's THE...ONLY...ONE...CLUB?" he asked with a mouth full of peanut butter. "Can I join?"

"You're not the only one of something, are you?" asked Jennifer.

"Maybe," said Jonah.

"What do you mean, maybe?"

"Maybe I am."

A minute later Jonah shouted, "I'm the only one in our class with red hair!"
Jennifer couldn't argue about that. Jonah McBride had the reddest hair she'd ever seen, with a gazillion matching freckles. "Hmmm," Jennifer said. "I have to think about it."
Jonah gave her a raspberry, spraying peanut butter all over the lunch table.

"What's that badge for?" Steven whispered to Jonah after lunch.

"It's for THE ONLY ONE CLUB," Jonah whispered back.

"Can I join?" asked Steven.

"Are you the only one?" Jonah asked back.

"The only one what?" Steven asked.

"The only one who's something that no one else is," Jonah explained, "but you'll have to ask Jennifer. She started the club and she's the only one in it."

"I want to be in it, too," Steven whined. "I must be the only one of something."

By the time afternoon recess was over everyone had asked
if they could join THE ONLY ONE CLUB and Jennifer didn't
know what to say.

Later, she overheard Olivia asking some kids if they wanted
to start a **NOT** THE ONLY ONE CLUB. Jennifer started to
feel sad.

When she got home from school Jennifer went straight to her room.
She knew what she needed to do.

The next day Jennifer lugged a large shoebox to school.

"What's in the box?" everyone asked.

"Line up in front of me and I'll show you," she announced.

Jennifer opened the box very slowly.
It was bursting with ONLY ONE CLUB badges.
"You can all be members of THE ONLY
ONE CLUB," Jennifer proclaimed
as she handed out badges,
"because...Alex Martin –
you're the only
one in our class
who was born
on a bus.

Niki and Nina –
you're the only
identical twins in
the whole school.

Jonah McBride – you have the reddest hair
and the most freckles of anyone in the class,
maybe even the whole universe." Jonah blushed
as red as his hair.
"Gwen Beacham – you're the only girl who wears a dress every single
day, with ribbons to match." Gwen twirled around and around.

"Sam Lee – you…are…the only one…with a pet iguana!
Julia Martinez – you're the only one who can jump
Double Dutch." Julia bounced
on her toes.

"Michael Baker – you are the only
first grader in the high math class.

Olivia Raven – you're the only one whose last name is a bird." Olivia smiled as she ran around the room flapping her arms.

"And Steven Whittier – you...are...the only one... who has all of his big, and I mean humongous, front teeth!" Steven just grinned.

Jennifer handed out badges until everyone in the class had one.
When Mrs. Matthews came in she faced a sea of glittery badges
and joyful smiles. "What's all this?" she asked.

"It's THE ONLY ONE CLUB," everyone yelled, "and we're
all members – because we're all THE ONLY ONES!"

Mrs. Matthews looked puzzled.

"You tell her, Jennifer," said Olivia. "You started it."

"I started the club because I was the only one who was Jewish," Jennifer explained. "But then everyone said **they** were the only ones of something. You're the only one here who isn't in our club, Mrs. Matthews, and since you're THE ONLY ONE, you can join too!"

Jennifer held out the biggest, most glittery badge of all.
Mrs. Matthews proudly pinned it to her blouse.

"I'm really glad everyone's the only one of something," Jennifer said.
"Me too, Jennifer," said Mrs. Matthews. "Me too."